The Spray-Paint Mystery

Other Scholastic titles
you will enjoy:

My Secret Valentine
Patricia Hermes

The Ghost Comes Calling
Betty Ren Wright

Fourth Grade Rats
Jerry Spinelli

The Spray-Paint Mystery

Angela Shelf Medearis

Illustrated by Richard Williams

A
LITTLE APPLE
PAPERBACK

SCHOLASTIC INC.
New York Toronto London Auckland Sydney

ISBN 0-590-48474-5

12   2/0

Printed in the U.S.A.   40

First Scholastic printing, December 1996

Contents

The Spray-Paint Mystery

1
The New Kid

"Third grade stinks," Cameron Thompson whispered to himself. He had been a third grader for two whole months and couldn't believe he'd been afraid to move from second to third grade. He'd worried all summer for no reason at all. What would happen if he couldn't do third-grade work? They would probably put him back into second grade — that's what. He'd be the biggest kid in the whole class. Everyone would make fun of him.

Now here he was, a big, bad third grader. Big deal.

Cameron was usually the first one to finish the reading assignment. Today, it had only taken eight minutes for him to answer all the questions at the end of the chapter. He'd timed himself. Everyone else was just now turning in their work. Third grade was nothing to be afraid of.

"Okay, class," Mrs. Sutton said. "Everyone has finished the reading assignment. Now, let's talk about something really old." She clipped a picture of a woolly mammoth to the board.

Cameron sat up straight. He loved prehistoric animals, and the woolly mammoth was one of his favorites.

"The mammoth was a part of the elephant family," Mrs. Sutton explained. "Some mammoths had tusks that were fifteen feet long and weighed as much as two-hundred fifty pounds."

Cameron quietly ducked his head under the top of his desk so Mrs. Sutton couldn't

2

see him. Then he turned around and smiled at his friend Jessie Rivas.

"I'm a mammoth," Cameron said. Two pencils hung out of his nose. "These are my tusks."

"Man, that's gross," Jessie whispered. "Better be careful. Those pencils are going to get stuck. You'll have to walk around like that forever."

The principal's voice crackled over the loudspeaker.

"Mrs. Sutton," said Mr. Garcia.

The speaker's buzzing sound made Cameron jump. The pencils wiggled up and down. They didn't fall out! Maybe they were stuck! The rest of the class started to giggle. Cameron yanked the pencils out as fast as he could.

Mrs. Sutton looked at him and rubbed her forehead. She always did that when she was getting a headache — usually three or four times a day.

"Be quiet, class," Mrs. Sutton said. "I can't hear."

3

" . . . send someone to the office. We have a new student who has been assigned to your room."

"I'll send someone right away," Mrs. Sutton said. "Cameron?"

"Yes?" Cameron said.

"Please go to the office. You may escort the new student to our classroom."

"Okay," Cameron said.

"And Cameron," Mrs. Sutton said, "you've been doing very well. But, please, no funny stuff for the rest of the day, okay?"

"I'm sorry, Mrs. Sutton," Cameron said.

"Okay," Mrs. Sutton said as she wrote out a hall pass.

Cameron took the pass and walked quickly down the hall. Mr. Murray, the janitor, was throwing a bag into the trash can. Suddenly, the bag split open. Can after can of red, green, and blue spray paint clattered to the floor and rolled down the hall. Cameron stopped to help him pick them up.

"Thanks," Mr. Murray said as he dropped the last can into the trash bin.

"Where did all those empty cans come from?" Cameron asked.

"Well," Mr. Murray said. "Someone painted graffiti on the wall behind the gym. They left those empty cans all over the ground. What a mess."

"Does anyone know who did it?" Cameron asked.

"No," Mr. Murray said. "It's a mystery."

Cameron started to smile. He loved mysteries. His father was a police detective. Cameron loved to hear about the cases his dad was working on.

"Maybe I can find out who's spray painting the walls," Cameron said. "I'm a third grader during the day, but at night I'm Super Detective!"

"Well, the case is yours, Mr. Super Detective," Mr. Murray said.

"Thanks, Mr. Murray. I'll do my best to solve it."

"I've cleaned a lot of graffiti in my time," Mr. Murray said. "But there was something strange about this paint job."

"What?"

"It looked like they changed their mind and tried to scrub some of the paint off."

"That's weird," Cameron said. "Why would they spray paint the wall and then try to scrub it off?"

"Beats me," said Mr. Murray. "You're the Super Detective. You figure it out. I'm going to sandblast that paint off the wall this afternoon."

"Can I have one of those empty spray cans?" Cameron asked.

"For what?"

"It's a clue," Cameron said.

"I'll hold it for you until after school," said Mr. Murray. "By the way, what are you doing in the hall?"

Cameron held up the hall pass.

"How did you win a free trip to the principal's office this time?"

"I'm going to get a new student who's coming to our class," Cameron explained.

"I see," said Mr. Murray.

"I've been behaving myself," Cameron

said. "I got a good-conduct sticker every day last week."

"That's wonderful," Mr. Murray said. "Keep up the good work. By the way, why was it that you had to go to the office the last time?"

"Well," Cameron said, "I got into trouble for tying the bow on Tarann Johnson's dress to her chair. Mrs. Sutton called on her to go to the blackboard and she dragged the chair halfway down the aisle. It was pretty funny."

Mr. Murray smiled. "You'd better get going. You don't want to keep Mr. Garcia waiting. Thanks again for your help. I'll see you after school."

"You're welcome," Cameron said. "I'll see you later."

Cameron ran down the hall.

"Walk, please," Mr. Murray shouted after him. "You know the rules."

Cameron slowed to a walk. He quietly pushed open the door to the principal's office.

"Cameron, Cameron, Cameron," said Miss Parker, the school secretary, with a smile. "What is it this time? Did you tie Tarann's dress to her chair again?"

"No, I'm here to get the new student," Cameron said. "I haven't played any jokes on Tarann for two whole weeks."

"Good for you," Miss Parker said. "Have a seat. Mr. Garcia will be with you in a minute."

Cameron sat down. He looked around the office. Someone's backpack and notebook were neatly stacked on the other end of the couch. The notebook was decorated with bright colors. Before Cameron could have a closer look, Mr. Garcia appeared.

"Cameron," Mr. Garcia said. "I thought we decided that we weren't going to see your lovely face in here again."

Mr. Garcia stood in front of Cameron and folded his arms. A small boy in a bright yellow jacket quickly picked up the notebook and backpack. He looked at Cameron shyly.

"Mrs. Sutton sent me to get the new student," Cameron explained.

"I see," said Mr. Garcia. He put his arm around the new boy. "Miguel Oliveras, meet Cameron Thompson. Miguel and his family are from Houston."

"That's where my mom lives," said Cameron. "She took me to Fun City. I rode the Shake Your Liver 'til It Quivers ride eight times."

"I like that ride, too," Miguel said.

"Well, it looks like you two have something in common," Mr. Garcia said. "Welcome to Austin, and to Pecan Springs Elementary School, Miguel. I'm sure you'll like it here. Cameron will introduce you to your teacher, Mrs. Sutton."

"Thanks," Miguel said.

"Come on," Cameron said. "I'll show you where our classroom is."

"Good luck, Miguel," Miss Parker said.

"Thank you," Miguel said.

"See you later," Cameron said to Mr. Garcia, smiling.

"I hope not," Mr. Garcia sighed.

"Do they have a soccer team here?" asked Miguel as they walked down the hall.

"Yeah," Cameron said. "We practice on Saturdays on the field behind the school. I love soccer."

"Me, too," Miguel said. "It's the best game there is."

Cameron smiled at him. "I think so, too. Give me five!"

Miguel raised his hand, and the smile slipped off Cameron's face. He looked at Miguel's hand. It was covered with streaks of red, blue, and green paint.

Oh no, Cameron thought to himself. The new kid is my main suspect in the Spray Paint Mystery.

2
Paint Problems

Cameron introduced Miguel to Mrs. Sutton.

"Welcome, Miguel," Mrs. Sutton said. "There's an empty desk next to Tyler."

Cameron thought fast. If Miguel sat next to him, he could keep an eye on him. "There's an empty desk next to mine, too," Cameron said quickly.

Miguel smiled happily.

"All right, we'll try it for awhile," Mrs.

Sutton said. "But if you two talk too much, Miguel will have to move."

"Okay," Cameron said.

As soon as Cameron reached his desk, he began to look for a piece of paper. He wanted to write Tarann a note. He would need her help to solve this case.

Cameron dug around his desk. It was a mess. He found an old orange, two rubber bands, and a broken crayon. But no paper. The orange was turning green. Cameron thought about throwing it away. Then he changed his mind. Maybe it would come in handy at lunch. He could ask if anyone had something they wanted to trade for an orange. Then he could pull that moldy orange out of his lunch bag. That would be a good joke.

Cameron put the moldy orange back inside his desk. Finally, he found a clean sheet of paper in one of his folders. Yes! Cameron thought for a moment, then began to write:

Dear Tarann:
I need your help! There's something
strange about this new kid Miguel.
Wait for me after school. I want to
show you something. It's a mystery.
    Your friend,
    Cameron, Super Detective

Cameron waited until Mrs. Sutton's back
was turned. Then he tapped Tarann on the
back with the note. She turned around and
looked at the note. Then she rolled her eyes.

"What did you do?" Tarann whispered.
"Wipe your nose on it first?"

"No," Cameron whispered back. "Take it.
It's important."

"This better not be a trick," Tarann said.
"Or else." She balled up her fist and shook
it at Cameron.

"No more tricks," Cameron said. "I
promise."

"Yeah, right," Tarann said. She carefully
took the note and read it.

"Okay," she whispered. "But only for a

minute. I need to hurry home. I've got to finish my science experiment."

"Okay," Cameron said. Yes!

Tarann turned back around and began copying the assignment off the board. She was one of the smartest kids in the third grade. She could add long rows of numbers together in her head. Her science projects usually won first place at the science fair. And best of all, she never smelled stinky. Even after she and Cameron played basketball all afternoon in the hot sun.

When the last bell rang, Cameron put his books in his backpack as quickly as he could. His math worksheet! Where in the world was his math worksheet? Tarann was already out the door before he could find it.

"What are you looking for?" Miguel asked.

"I can't find my math worksheet," Cameron answered.

"I'm through with mine," Miguel said. "I've already worked out the problems in my notebook. You can have it if you want it."

"Great," Cameron said.

Miguel opened his backpack. Cameron could see the tops of two brightly colored plastic cans. Spray paint! Miguel quickly took out the worksheet and zipped up the backpack.

"What's that in your backpack?" Cameron asked. He tried to take the backpack out of Miguel's hand.

"Nothing," Miguel answered as he jerked it away. "I've got to go."

"Hey!" Cameron said. Miguel ran out of the room and down the hall. Cameron started to run after him.

"Cameron," Mrs. Sutton said. "Wait just a minute."

"Oh, man," Cameron groaned. "Now what did I do?"

"You've been fine," Mrs. Sutton said. "I have a note I'd like you to take home to your father. I want to remind him about speaking to our school for Career Day."

"Oh, yeah," Cameron said, relieved. "I forgot about that."

"Here you are," Mrs. Sutton said. "See you tomorrow."

"Bye," Cameron said. He ran as fast as he could down the hall. Miguel was nowhere in sight. Then he remembered Tarann. Cameron had forgotten all about meeting her! He raced through the doors. Tarann was waiting for him by the bike racks.

"Hi, Tarann," Cameron said. "Sorry I'm late."

Before he knew what was happening, Tarann punched him in the arm as hard as she could.

"Ow!" Cameron shouted. "What was that for?"

"That was for the tricks you played on the teacher in the first grade and blamed on me!"

"Man, that hurt," Cameron said as he rubbed his arm.

"Okay, I'm sorry," Tarann said. "But

18

everyone laughed at me for a whole year because of you!"

"I said I was sorry," Cameron said.

"Okay, okay. Now we're even," Tarann said. "What's the big deal?"

"I need your help to solve a mystery," Cameron said.

"What mystery?" Tarann asked. "How you made it to third grade?"

"Come on, Tarann," Cameron said. "Just listen to me. Someone spray painted the wall behind the gym."

"I know," Tarann said. "I can see that wall from my bedroom window."

"Did you see anything strange last night?"

"No," Tarann said. "I sure didn't."

"I was hoping you had," Cameron said. "I think that new kid in our class is the one who did it."

"Miguel?" Tarann said. "What makes you think he did it?"

"He had paint on his hands. Also, I saw two cans of spray paint in his backpack."

"That doesn't mean he spray painted the wall."

"They were the same colors as the paint cans Mr. Murray picked up near the wall," Cameron said.

"Yeah, but all he has to do is wash his hands or hide the cans. If his hands are clean and the cans are gone, there goes your case."

"I know," Cameron said, "but right now he's my main suspect."

"You're going to need more than a pair of dirty hands to prove he's the spray painter."

"Whose side are you on, anyway?"

"I'm not picking a side. I'll make up my mind when I see some evidence."

"Let's go look at the wall," Cameron said. "Maybe there are some more clues there."

"Race you," Tarann said.

She started running as soon as the words were out of her mouth. Cameron struggled to catch up. Tarann ran down the hill at top speed.

Just when Cameron thought he was gaining on Tarann, he tripped. He rolled down the hill, head over heels, like a bowling ball. He finally came to a stop at the bottom of the hill, but the world was still spinning.

"Beat you!" Tarann said, laughing. She pulled Cameron to his feet and helped him brush the grass out of his hair and off his clothes. Even though Cameron and Tarann teased each other, they were still best friends.

"Man, you cheated. You started running before I knew what was going on."

"That's my secret for winning," Tarann said, tossing her long braids over her shoulders. "I like to get a head start."

"Come on," Cameron said. "Let's go look at the wall."

Tarann and Cameron walked from one end of the brick wall to the other. Huge symbols, strange words, and pictures of people and animals covered the wall from top to bottom.

"I hate to say this," Tarann said. "But whoever did this can really draw."

"Yeah," Cameron said. "But they should draw on paper instead of messing up our neighborhood."

"That's true," Tarann said. "Well, I don't see anything that looks like a clue."

"Wait a minute," Cameron said. He knelt down near the edge of the wall.

"What is it?" Tarann leaned over to have a closer look.

"See this?" Cameron pointed to an odd symbol. Two zeros with a thumbprint in the middle had been placed at the bottom of the wall. "It looks like two eyes and a nose."

"That's probably how this guy signs his work," Tarann said. "You know, instead of writing his name, he draws this face thing. It's called a tag."

"What we need is a picture of this thumbprint," Cameron said. "It could be a great clue."

"I got a camera for my birthday," Tarann said. "I'll run home and get it. I'll take a whole roll of pictures. Then tomorrow we can take the film to Welberts' SuperStore. They can develop it in an hour."

"Maybe we could get a thumbprint from Miguel and see if it matches the print on the wall," Cameron suggested.

"That's a great idea," Tarann said.

"We can look at both prints under the fingerprint glass in my dad's kit. That's what they do at the police station. I've seen them. If the thumbprints match, we have proof that Miguel did this. I'll see if I can borrow my dad's fingerprint kit."

"Okay, but how are you going to get Miguel's thumbprint without him catching on?" Tarann asked.

"I'll think of something," Cameron said. "We need to work fast, though. Mr. Murray is going to clean this wall as soon as he finishes mopping."

"I'll go get my camera right now," Tarann said.

"Hey," a loud voice shouted, "what are you kids doing?" A tall, skinny teenager stood near the end of the wall. His dark blue eyes looked mean.

"Nothing," Cameron said. "We were just looking."

"Yeah?" the boy said. "Well take a good look because that wall was done by the GQ Posse. They're not anyone to be messing with."

Cameron knew all about gangs from listening to his father.

"I know the signs," Cameron said.

"Well let me tell you something else you should know," the boy said. He towered over Cameron and glared down at him. His pale face was only a few inches from Cameron's. "I don't ever want to see you near this wall again."

Cameron took a step back and almost tripped over Tarann.

"Come on, Cameron," Tarann said as she tugged on his arm. "I've got to go home."

"Okay," Cameron stammered.

"Yeah," the boy said, scowling. "Beat it."

Cameron and Tarann ran back up the hill as fast as they could.

"Man," Tarann said. "He looked like Count Dracula's cousin."

"I know," Cameron said. "I wonder who he is and what he's doing hanging around the wall."

"Maybe I can take a picture of him from my bedroom window."

"That's a good idea," Cameron said. "But be careful. That guy looks mean."

"After I take his picture, I'll wait until he's gone and then come back and take some pictures of that thumbprint. You want to come over for awhile?"

"Sorry, Tarann," Cameron said. "I've got to go. I need to get that spray can from Mr. Murray. Then I need to go home and start cooking dinner."

"Okay. I'll see you later. I'll let you know how everything goes."

"See you tomorrow," Cameron shouted as he ran back up the hill and into the school.

He hurried down the hall to the mainte-
nance room. Mr. Murray was inside, filling
up his mop bucket.

"So," Mr. Murray said, "the Super Detective returns! How did you get all that
grass in your hair?"

"I tripped," Cameron said. "Can I have
that empty can now?"

"Sure," Mr. Murray said as he handed it
to Cameron. "Find any more clues?"

"Well, maybe a few," Cameron said. "I'll
let you know tomorrow. I've gotta run. It's
my day to start dinner."

"No running, remember?" Mr. Murray
said.

"Okay," Cameron said. "Gotta walk then!
See you later."

Some kindergarten students were walk-
ing down the hall. They always reminded
Cameron of the little people in *The Wizard
of Oz*.

"Excuse me, excuse me," Cameron said.
"I need to get by."

"What's your hurry, Cameron?" Mr. Garcia, the principal, was leaning against the wall.

"I just need to get home," Cameron said.

"What's that in your hand?" Mr. Garcia asked.

"This?" Cameron held up the empty spray can.

"Yes, that," Mr. Garcia said.

"It's a spray paint can."

"I know that!" Mr. Garcia said. "Someone painted the wall behind the gym last night."

"I know," Cameron said.

"Well," Mr. Garcia said. "I think that someone was you. Come into my office. I want to talk to you."

3
Trouble

"I didn't do anything, Mr. Garcia," Cameron said.

"Then what are you doing with that can of spray paint?"

"It's a clue," Cameron said.

"A clue?"

"Yes, sir. See, I'm working on the Spray Paint Mystery."

Mr. Garcia leaned back in his chair and looked at Cameron for a long time.

"Okay," Mr. Garcia said. "Tell me the whole story from the beginning."

"Well," Cameron said, "this morning, Mr. Murray dropped a bunch of spray paint cans in the hall. I helped him pick them up. Then he told me that someone had spray painted the wall behind the gym. I offered to take the case. I've already got two suspects and a few clues."

"So now you're a detective?"

"And I want to be a good one," Cameron said. "Just like my dad."

"Okay, Cameron," Mr. Garcia said. "You can go now. I was going to call your father tonight, anyway. I need his help with this problem and a few other things. It looks like a new gang is moving into the area. I guess there's already one Detective Thompson on this case. It won't hurt to have two. Make sure you tell your dad what you're doing."

"Yes, sir. I'll tell him tonight."

Cameron picked up his backpack and headed for the door.

"Cameron?"

"Yes?"

"If there is even one report about you misbehaving in class, you're off the case. Understand?"

"I understand," Cameron said.

"Good luck," Mr. Garcia said.

"Thanks." Cameron smiled. "See you tomorrow."

Cameron took a shortcut through the gym. His shoes squeaked loudly as he walked across the huge room. It always smelled exactly the same, a combination of sweat and stinky feet. Cameron jumped as high as he could, but wasn't even close to touching the basketball rim. Oh, well, it doesn't matter how tall you are when you play soccer. He kicked an imaginary ball out of the gym and into the hall.

Cameron slowed down to look at the artwork on display in the main hallway. Art was one of Cameron's favorite subjects, next to reading. Mrs. Carter, the art teacher, was still in her room. Nicky Viceroy was getting art supplies out of a cabinet. Nicky was in the fifth grade. He was one of the best artists in the whole school.

"Hey, Mrs. Carter. What's up, Nicky?"

Nicky and Cameron slapped hands.

"Hi, Cameron," Mrs. Carter said. "Can you help us move this cardboard?"

"Sure," Cameron said.

Cameron helped them stack the huge sheets of cardboard against the wall. It was hot, dusty work.

"We've got to get all the scenery put together and painted for the fifth-grade play by next Friday."

"Looks like there's still a lot to be done," Cameron said.

"There sure is," Mrs. Carter said. "I haven't gotten very much help, either."

"Well," Cameron said. "I'll help you as much as I can."

"That would be wonderful," Mrs. Carter said. "Nicky has been helping me every day after school."

"I've been spray painting the background scenery," Nicky said. He held up a can of spray paint and smiled.

Cameron looked at the paint can. It was just like the one he had in his backpack.

"Spray painting the background was Nicky's idea," Mrs. Carter said. "He's really good at it. Looks nice, doesn't it?"

Cameron stared at the bright red paint. It was the same shade as the red paint on the brick wall near the playground.

"What are you staring at?" Nicky asked.

"It looks great," Cameron said quickly. "Do you have any empty spray paint cans?"

"There are a couple in the trash," Nicky said.

"Why do you want an empty can?" Mrs. Carter asked. She looked at Cameron like he had lost his mind.

"It's an experiment I'm doing," Cameron said. "You know, some kids study bugs. I like spray paint cans."

Nicky looked at Cameron suspiciously. Cameron started to sweat.

"That's the weirdest hobby I've ever heard of," Mrs. Carter said. "But help yourself."

Cameron dug around in the trash until he found an empty can. But when he turned to go, Nicky blocked his way.

"I don't think you collect empty cans," Nicky said. "I think you're up to something."

"Yeah, so what? Move out of my way, man," Cameron said. "I've got to get home."

"Nicky," Mrs. Carter said. "Let's get back to work. Thanks for your help, Cameron."

"You're welcome," Cameron said.

Nicky didn't say anything. He watched Cameron as he walked down the hall. Cameron looked over his shoulder. Nicky was still watching him from the doorway of the art room. Cameron pushed through the doors to the outside and headed toward home.

Trouble, trouble, trouble. This case was turning into nothing but trouble. And boy, Cameron sure had his share of troubles lately.

First, his mom and dad decided to get a divorce last year. His mom talked to him for a long time about why she was leaving. She tried to explain why it was best for Cameron to stay with his dad. She said she didn't want him to have to start over at a new school. Cameron said he understood, but he really didn't. Then his mom moved to Houston.

Cameron still got a chance to see her during the summer, and on school holidays, but it wasn't the same. Now, he had to do a lot of things around the house that his mom used to do. When his dad worked the night shift, Cameron had to have a baby-sitter. Most of the time, he stayed at Tar-ann's house. Her mother kept an eye on him until his dad got home from work.

For a long time, Cameron thought his mom left because he was bad. Or because he hardly ever cleaned his room like she told him to. Then, it seemed like he started getting into trouble all the time at school.

Mr. Garcia had a long talk with his dad. After that, it seemed like his dad was at home more. He hugged Cameron and told

34

him that he'd always be there to take care of him. It made Cameron feel a little better, but he still missed his mom.

Everything was different now. Cameron didn't like it at all. He spent the summers in Houston with his mom. The rest of the year, he lived with his dad. He hated going back and forth between the two of them. Why couldn't they get back together? Cameron just didn't understand it.

Cameron switched his backpack to his other shoulder. The empty paint cans clanked together, reminding him of the mystery. Suddenly, Cameron had an idea.

He dug the cans out of his backpack and looked at them closely. The same sticker was on the bottom of each can. Welberts' SuperStore! Maybe one of the store clerks would remember who they'd sold spray paint to recently if Cameron described Miguel, Nicky, and the skinny guy who looked like Count Dracula. That would be just the break he needed.

An empty soft drink can lay on the sidewalk. Cameron kicked the can from one side of the walk to the other. He practiced his best soccer moves as the can bounced down the street. He pretended he was playing in front of a huge crowd.

"Now," Cameron said, "here's the game winning point!"

Cameron kicked the can as hard as he could. It sailed through the air.

Two boys were sitting on the steps of an apartment building at the end of the block. Cameron watched helplessly as the can soared in their direction. As if in slow motion, the can turned end over end and began to fall. It was going to hit one of the boys!

"Look out!" Cameron shouted.

It was too late. With a loud thump, the can bounced off the head of the older boy. The can clattered down the steps and rolled across the ground. It stopped at Cameron's feet.

The boy rubbed his head. He slowly stood up. He was huge, and mad.

"You think you're funny, don't you?" the

boy said as he walked over to Cameron.

Cameron was so scared that he couldn't move. He couldn't even speak.

The boy picked up Cameron by the back of his jacket and shook him a few times. Cameron's head rattled until he was dizzy.

"Well, we'll see who's the funniest. Try laughing after I make you swallow some of those big teeth of yours."

The boy drew back his fist. It looked like the huge ham his mother baked once for Easter dinner. Cameron had never seen a fist that big.

Cameron closed his eyes. He was dead meat and he knew it.

4
Help From a Friend

Cameron waited for the punch. He pictured himself with a black eye, a busted nose, and swollen lips. Tears welled up in his eyes. Everyone would laugh at him. He braced himself for the pain. Nothing happened. Cameron slowly opened one of his eyes. Miguel was hanging from the boy's arm so that he couldn't hit him!

"Put him down, Oscar," Miguel said. "He didn't mean to do it."

"You better let go of me, Miguel," Oscar said. "Or else I'll punch you, too."

But Miguel still hung on.

"Mama! Mama!" Miguel screamed. "Oscar's fighting again!"

A door flew open. A tiny woman came outside.

"Oscar Oliveras," said the woman. "Put that boy down, *pronto*."

Oscar threw Cameron to the ground. Cameron landed flat on his back. His head bounced on the sidewalk.

"Oops," Oscar said. "My fingers slipped."

Oscar's mother said something to him in Spanish. Cameron couldn't understand what she said, but he knew Oscar was in big trouble.

"I'll take care of you later," Oscar whispered. "I'm coming, Mama."

Oscar ran up the steps, two at a time. Mrs. Oliveras grabbed him by the arm and pushed him inside.

"Are you hurt?" Miguel asked, helping Cameron stand up.

Cameron's head was throbbing. The pain seemed to move around and around his skull like a model train going around a track.

"You don't look so good," Miguel said. "You better come and sit down."

Miguel helped Cameron up the steps and into the house. Mrs. Oliveras grabbed Cameron's other arm and helped him sit down. She patted his cheek and gently touched the bruise on the back of his head.

"Oh, you poor thing," Mrs. Oliveras said. "Look at the lump on your head. That Oscar! I'll get some ice."

She hurried away. Cameron heard the freezer door open and the clink of ice. Miguel put a pillow behind his head.

"I know you didn't mean to hit Oscar with that can," Miguel said. "He has a bad temper."

"He sure does," Cameron agreed.

"You better try to stay out of his way," Miguel said. "He's nothing but trouble. He's always getting into fights."

"Great," Cameron said. "Your brother sounds like the Terminator."

"That's his nickname," Miguel said.

"Oh, no," Cameron said. He leaned back against the pillow and closed his eyes. He probably wouldn't live to see the fourth grade with the Terminator on his trail.

"He has a brown belt in karate," Miguel said. "Back when he was in fifth grade, he knocked out a senior in high school with one punch."

"Oscar knocked someone out when he was only ten years old?" Cameron asked, amazed. He slumped against the pillow. "I'm dead. He's going to kill me."

"I don't think so," Miguel said. "He'll probably just hurt you a little."

Cameron moaned softly and covered his eyes.

"He's already six feet tall and he's only in the tenth grade," Miguel said. "He wears a size-thirteen shoe."

"Don't tell me anything else," Cameron said. "I've heard enough."

"Well," Miguel said, "the good news is that he doesn't hold a grudge very long."

"Good," Cameron said. He felt a little better.

"He'll probably forget all about what you did to him in about six weeks."

"Six weeks!"

"Yeah," Miguel said, "but it could be worse."

"I don't see how," Cameron groaned.

"Well, that can could have hit my other brother, Antonio," Miguel said. "He's even bigger than Oscar."

Mrs. Oliveras bustled back into the room. She was holding a towel filled with ice.

"Here you go," Mrs. Oliveras said as she pressed the ice pack against Cameron's head. "This will make that swelling go down."

"Thank you," Cameron said. The ice made his head feel better.

"I made some *empanadas*," Mrs. Oliveras said. "Would you like one?"

"What are they?" Cameron asked.

"A Mexican pastry — *empanadas* are sort of like little fried pies."

43

"They're good," Miguel said.

Mrs. Oliveras smiled at Miguel. "They're his favorite dessert."

"Okay," Cameron said. "I'll try one."

"Come on," Mrs. Oliveras said. "They're in the kitchen."

Oscar was sitting at the kitchen table. He had an *empanada* in each hand and his mouth was full. The plate was empty.

"Oscar!" Mrs. Oliveras said. "There were at least half a dozen *empanadas* left. I can't believe you ate all of them."

"I can," Miguel said. "He eats everything."

"You'd better apologize to our guest right now for your rude behavior and for being so greedy."

"Sorry," Oscar mumbled. He didn't look like he was sorry, though.

"I've had enough," Mrs. Oliveras said. "Go to your room and don't come out until I tell you to."

Oscar wiped his mouth on his sleeve and glared at Cameron. The wooden floor trembled as he lumbered down the hallway.

"I'm sorry, Cameron," Mrs. Oliveras said. "I'll make some more *empanadas* especially for you."

"That's okay, Mrs. Oliveras," Cameron said. "I need to be going anyway."

Cameron picked up his backpack and headed home. He gently rubbed the back of his head. The lump was still there, but it didn't hurt as much. Suddenly, a loud noise caught his attention. Cameron spun around. Oscar had opened his bedroom window and climbed out! He'd overturned a trash can when he jumped to the ground.

"I'm going to get you for getting me into trouble, you little jerk," Oscar screamed.

He began to run after Cameron. Cameron's feet seemed to have a mind of their own. Before he knew it, he was running faster than he had ever run before. His heart was pounding and sweat poured down his face. Seven blocks before he could reach the house and safety. He'd never make it alive.

Cameron looked over his shoulder. Oscar was gaining on him with every step he took in those size-thirteen tennis shoes. Cameron had never seen anyone so big or so angry.

Wham! The next thing Cameron knew, he was flat on his back for the second time that day.

Cameron slowly sat up and stared at the shiny black shoes in front of him. They looked familiar — so did the navy blue pants, the belt buckle, and the dark blue jacket.

"Dad!"

Oscar skidded to a stop and almost tripped over Cameron. He looked frightened when he saw Mr. Thompson's police uniform. He tried to casually walk around Cameron's father.

"Not so fast," Mr. Thompson said as he grabbed Oscar's arm. "What's the problem here?"

"Nothing, Dad," Cameron said quickly. "Oscar and I were just racing."

Oscar looked at Cameron as if he'd lost his mind.

"Didn't look that way to me," Mr. Thompson said. "It looked like you were running for your life."

"No, sir," Cameron said. "I was just running."

"You look familiar," Mr. Thompson said. He stared at Oscar as if he were trying to remember something.

"We're new around here," Oscar said. "I've got to be going now." He backed away and then hurried down the street.

"I know I've seen that face before," Mr. Thompson said.

"It's no big deal, Dad," Cameron said.

"Maybe it's not," Mr. Thompson said. "But the fact that you're over an hour and a half late getting home is. You know what I told you would happen if you came home late again. Let's go."

Cameron rubbed the lump on his head. This had been one of the longest days of his life, and it was only 5:30.

5
Spaghetti Night

Last week, Cameron's dad told him that if he was late one more time, he'd be grounded. But after Cameron explained everything that had happened to him that day, his dad changed his mind.

"Looks like you've had enough punishment for one day," he said. "Let me see that knot on your head."

Cameron pointed to the lump on the back of his head.

"I guess I'd better get used to taking lumps if I'm going to be a detective like you." Cameron smiled at his father.

His dad looked at Cameron for a long time. Then he smiled and swung Cameron around until he was dizzy. He hadn't swung Cameron around since he was little. It made Cameron feel good.

As soon as they got home, Cameron washed his hands and started dinner. Tonight was spaghetti night. Cameron loved making spaghetti. He loved to make it almost as much as he loved to eat it.

Cameron put a pot of water on to boil. Then he carefully dropped in two handfuls of spaghetti. Next, he opened a jar of spaghetti sauce and poured it into a bowl. He added some spices and stirred them in. Then he put the sauce in the microwave to warm it up.

His father rustled around in the refrigerator. He pulled out a head of lettuce, some carrots, and tomatoes. He rinsed the lettuce and began tearing the leaves into bite-size pieces. Then he took an onion out of the bin and put it on the chopping board.

"I hope you're wrong about Miguel," Mr. Thompson said as he sliced the tomatoes. "But kids get involved with gangs at younger and younger ages now."

"I hope he's not in a gang, either," Cameron said. "I like him, but I hate seeing all that graffiti everywhere. It makes the neighborhood look bad."

"My new partner and I have been taking pictures of the graffiti on the walls around town," Mr. Thompson said. "I don't remember ever seeing a sign that used two zeros and a thumbprint."

"Must be a new guy then," Cameron said. He had a sudden thought. "I forgot to tell you about two other suspects I have."

"Who?"

"One's Nicky Viceroy," Cameron said. "He's the one who had the spray paint in the art room."

"I know Nicky," Mr. Thompson said. "He got into trouble over the summer. He was writing graffiti on the side of a vacant building. But his tag wasn't a double zero and a thumbprint. I don't think he was in a gang. I got him enrolled into a summer art program. The last time I talked to him, he was doing fine. I hope he's not getting into trouble again."

"I don't know," Cameron said. "But he didn't look too happy about me taking that empty can."

"He could have joined a gang at the beginning of the school year," Mr. Thompson said. "If he did, double zero could be his new tag."

"I sure hope he hasn't done anything like that," Cameron said.

"Me, too. Who's your other suspect?"

"It's an older guy I've never seen before. He told us to stay away from the wall. He said it was the work of the GQ Posse. How would he know all that if he didn't do it?"

"You could be right," Mr. Thompson said. "But I'll need some more information to see if we have a file on him."

"Tarann got a fancy camera for her birthday. She was going to try to take a picture of him from her bedroom window. She's also going to take pictures of the wall and that double zero and thumbprint tag."

"Sounds like a good plan. Good thinking, Detective Thompson."

"Thanks."

Cameron stirred the spaghetti and lifted out a piece. He tasted it to see if it was done. His mother always let him test the spaghetti. Cameron used to gag and pretend that he was eating a worm to gross her out. His mom always laughed when he did that.

A wave of sadness passed over Cameron. He always seemed to miss his mother the most at dinnertime. The phone rang and Cameron raced to answer it.

"Hi, Cameron. This is Mr. Garcia. Is your dad at home?"

"Yes, sir," Cameron said. "Dad, Mr. Garcia's on the phone."

Cameron handed the phone to his father, then he started to slice some carrots for the salad. He could hear the deep rumble of his father's voice as he talked to Mr. Garcia. Cameron tossed the carrots, tomatoes, and lettuce together. He put the onion back into the bin. His dad liked onions, but Cameron didn't. He always pretended he forgot to put them in the salad.

Mr. Thompson hung up the phone. He got two plates out of the cabinet.

"Seems like Mr. Garcia has his hands full," Mr. Thompson said. "These gang members are recruiting younger and younger kids. He thinks that whoever painted the graffiti on the school wall may have done it to be part of a gang."

"Gangs are stupid," Cameron said. "They just get kids into trouble."

Cameron put a huge spoonful of sauce on his spaghetti and ate a bite. It was wonderful! Almost as good as Mom's.

"Well, most kids join gangs because they want to belong somewhere," Mr. Thompson said. He tasted the spaghetti. "Hey, this is good, Cameron."

"Thanks." Cameron smiled. "Do you

think we can go by Tarann's house and Welberts' SuperStore tomorrow?"

"Why?"

"I want to get Tarann's film developed at Welberts'. I also want to talk to the paint clerk. Maybe he'll remember seeing Miguel or Nicky buying spray paint. And once the film's developed, we can show the paint clerk a picture of that other guy I told you about. Whoever spray painted the wall had to buy at least eight or ten cans of paint."

"I guess I can take you. I don't have to go to work until midnight tomorrow. I was going to ask Mrs. Johnson if you could stay over there anyway."

"That will work out great."

"Good. I'll load up the dishes now. Go on and finish your homework. Then take a bath and get ready for bed."

"Okay," Cameron said. " 'Night, Dad."

"Good night. Holler if you need any help with your homework."

"I will."

Cameron ran upstairs to his room. He

struggled through his math worksheet. He always had trouble with division problems. Finally, he was finished. Cameron hoped the problems were right. His dad always looked over his homework before he went to bed. If it was wrong, Cameron would have to do the problems again. He hated doing them over! He always tried to make sure they were right the first time.

Cameron went into his father's room and put his math worksheet on the bed. Then he went into the bathroom. He sniffed under both arms. He didn't smell too bad. Cameron started the shower, jumped in, turned around, and jumped back out. He dried himself off and put on a clean T-shirt and underwear. No sense in wasting soap and water if he didn't stink.

Cameron got into bed. He picked up the book he'd been reading. He was on chapter eight of *Great Moments in Soccer History*. He loved reading about soccer almost as much as he loved playing it. Cameron felt warm and sleepy from all the excitement and the spaghetti. He yawned and closed his eyes for a minute. The next thing he knew, it was morning.

Cameron looked at the clock — 7:30 A.M.! He was going to be late for school. He kicked back the covers and stumbled into his father's room. Mr. Thompson was snoring loudly. Cameron started to wake him up for work. Then he remembered his father's schedule had been switched to the night shift. That was close. His father was always grouchy in the morning. He would have been really mad if Cameron woke him up for no reason.

Cameron began to tiptoe out of the room. He was almost to the door when he remembered his homework. His father always put it on top of his dresser when he was finished looking at it. Cameron quietly picked it up and headed for the door. Suddenly, his father let out an earsplitting snore that sounded like a bear with a bad cold. Cameron began to giggle. He bit his thumb to keep from laughing out loud. Thumbs. The fingerprint kit! He'd forgotten to tell his dad about getting Miguel's thumbprint to see if it matched the one on the wall. He would need to fingerprint Nicky, too. That wouldn't be easy. Nicky already thought he was up to something. Cameron sat on the edge of the bed and looked at his father.

If he woke up his father to ask him about borrowing the kit, he'd probably be mad. But if Cameron took the kit without asking him first, he'd be mad, too. Cameron crept up to the side of the bed. His father twitched in his sleep and started snoring again.

"Dad," Cameron whispered. "Is it okay if I borrow your fingerprinting kit? Snore if it's okay."

His dad snorted, turned over, and snored even louder.

"Thanks, Dad."

Cameron tiptoed over to the closet and got the kit down from the shelf. Then he hurried into his room to get dressed for school.

While he was dressing, Cameron tried to figure out a way to fingerprint his suspects. He couldn't think of anything. Maybe Tarann would have an idea. Cameron slid the kit into his backpack. Then he raced down the stairs and out the door.

Halfway to school, Cameron started smiling. He knew a way to get the fingerprints he needed. This scheme was so brilliant he'd probably get an *A* for the day! Cameron began to run faster. Just as he got to the playground, the tardy bell rang. He ran down the hall. Before he could sit down, Mrs. Sutton grabbed his arm.

"Cameron," Mrs. Sutton said. "You're late. Do you have a written excuse?"

"No, Mrs. Sutton."

"Then you'll need to go to the office and get a tardy slip."

Cameron began to sweat. Mr. Garcia told him if he didn't stay out of trouble, he was off the case. Mr. Garcia hated for anyone to be tardy.

"Let me explain why I'm late, Mrs. Sutton. I was working on a project you asked me to do."

Mrs. Sutton looked puzzled. "What project?"

"It's about the note you sent home to my dad yesterday."

"Okay, Cameron," Mrs. Sutton said. "I'm listening. But you'd better have a good excuse. If not, you're going straight to the principal's office."

6
Cameron's Plan

"Well," Cameron said, "I was late because I was getting some equipment from my dad. I wanted to show the kids what a real detective does."

"Why didn't you wait until tomorrow, so you could do it as part of Career Day?" Mrs. Sutton asked.

Cameron looked at Tarann. She had her head in her hands. She peeked at Cameron between her fingers.

"Well," Cameron said, "I thought we

could take thumbprints from some of the kids. Then tomorrow my dad could explain how they match a person's fingerprints to a crime scene. It took me a while to get my dad's fingerprinting kit. That's why I was late to school today."

"What a great idea." Mrs. Sutton smiled. "Class, as you know, tomorrow morning we're having our Career Day assembly. Cameron's father is our guest speaker. He's a police detective. Fingerprints often help the police solve crimes."

"Do you think I can fingerprint a few kids?" Cameron asked.

"Sure," Mrs. Sutton said. "You can take some time before recess to get the fingerprints you need."

"Would it be all right if I took some fingerprints from kids in other classes, too?"

"Sure," Mrs. Sutton said. "The whole school is coming to the Career Day assembly. I'll give you a hall pass and a note that explains what you're doing."

"Thanks." Cameron slid into his seat. Man, Cameron thought. I was almost busted.

Tarann waited until Mrs. Sutton's back was turned and gave him two thumbs-up.

"Good thinking," she whispered. "I thought you were history."

Cameron smiled. "So did I."

Now getting the fingerprints he needed would be easy. He looked at Miguel. His head was resting on his hand and his eyes were closed. He was asleep. Cameron stared at him for a moment. Then he got out his ruler and poked Miguel in the side.

"Wake up, man," Cameron whispered. "Didn't you go to bed last night?"

Miguel didn't answer or look at Cameron. He pulled out his notebook and hid behind the cover.

Cameron stared at the notebook. It had the same huge symbols, strange words, and pictures of people and animals that were on the wall behind the gym.

Miguel noticed that Cameron was looking at his notebook. He slammed it shut. Then he quickly put it inside his desk.

More evidence, Cameron thought. All I need are Miguel's thumbprints to wrap this case up.

At first, Cameron thought he would be happy to solve his first case. Now, he felt kind of sad. He didn't want Miguel to get into trouble. He remembered how Miguel protected him from Oscar. He thought about how nice Mrs. Oliveras was. She would be very upset when she found out Miguel was in trouble. Cameron didn't know what to do. It was his job to turn in all the evidence to Mr. Garcia. Maybe he could ask him to give Miguel another chance. Or maybe Miguel wasn't guilty. Maybe Nicky Viceroy was the guilty one. He sure had been acting funny lately. Or it could even be that scary guy who was by the wall yesterday.

A note dropped on Cameron's desk. It was from Tarann.

Dear Super Detective:
Please tell Mrs. Sutton you need some
help getting the fingerprints. Pick me, Okay?
                    Tarann
P.S. I shot a whole roll of film. I took
pictures with my new zoom lens of that
guy we saw by the wall! It works just
like a telescope! Maybe we can go to
Welberts' later. They can develop the
film while we wait.

Tarann smiled at him. The rest of the
morning flew by.

A few minutes before the bell rang for
recess, Cameron took the fingerprinting kit
out of his backpack and raised his hand.

"Mrs. Sutton," Cameron said. "Can I
start now?"

"Sure," Mrs. Sutton said. "This is such a
neat idea!"

"I'm going to need some help," Cameron
said.

Hands begin waving wildly in the air. Cameron looked around like he was thinking.

"Can Tarann help me?" Cameron asked.

"Of course," Mrs. Sutton said.

"Aw, man," said Jessie. "That's cold. I thought we were tight."

"Sorry," Cameron said. "I need her help."

Jessie frowned. "Oh, so it's like that, huh?"

"We'll take your thumbprints first, Jessie," Tarann said.

"Yeah," Cameron said. "Give me your hands."

Jessie started to smile. Cameron carefully inked each thumb and pressed them onto a clean sheet of white paper. Tarann wrote Jessie's name and the date under the prints.

"Okay," Cameron said. "Now we need someone else."

"Me, me!" shouted Victoria Rausch as she waved both hands in the air. "I want to do it."

"Would you chill?" Cameron said.

"How about Miguel?" Tarann asked.

"Great idea," Cameron said. "Let me have your hands, Miguel."

"That's okay," Miguel said. "Victoria can take my turn.

"Yeah," Victoria said. "Thanks, Miguel!"

Cameron sighed. "Okay, give me your hands."

Victoria held out her hands.

"Come on, Cameron," Tarann said.

"Okay, okay," Cameron said. He quickly inked each one of Victoria's thumbs.

"Now," Cameron said as he grabbed Miguel's hands, "we'll do yours."

"That's okay," Miguel said. He tried to take his hands away.

Cameron held on tightly and quickly began inking Miguel's thumbs.

"It's no problem," Cameron said. "See, all done."

Miguel stared at his inky thumbs. Then he looked at Cameron sadly. Cameron looked away. Miguel made him feel guilty,

like he had done something wrong.

"May we have that note now, Mrs. Sutton?" Tarann asked. "We need a few more prints."

"Sure," Mrs. Sutton said. "Meet us out on the playground when you've finished."

"We won't be long," Cameron said.

Cameron and Tarann walked quickly down the hall. Nicky Viceroy was in Mrs. Fergins's class. Mrs. Fergins read Mrs. Sutton's note and called the class to order.

"Attention please, class," Mrs. Fergins said. "Cameron's father is a detective. He will be coming to our school for Career Day. He's going to talk to us about fingerprinting and other ways detectives solve crimes. He needs a few fingerprints to use as examples."

"Me! Me!" Azure Hawkins shouted. "I want to do it."

A few other kids also raised their hands. Nicky Viceroy sat slouched in his seat. Both hands were shoved into his pockets.

"How many sets of prints do you need?" Mrs. Fergins asked.

"Just a couple," Cameron said.

"Okay, Azure," Mrs. Fergins said. She scratched her head and folded her arms. "Now we need one more. How about . . . "

"Nicky Viceroy," Cameron said quickly. "So we'll have one girl and one boy."

"That's fine," Mrs. Fergins said. "Come on up, Azure and Nicky."

Azure eagerly raced up to Mrs. Fergins's desk. Nicky slowly rose from his seat. He frowned at Cameron as he walked up to the front of the class.

Cameron and Tarann quickly took Azure's and Nicky's thumbprints. The bell rang for recess.

"Okay, everyone," Mrs. Fergins said. "Line up."

Chairs scraped against the floor and desktops slammed closed as the students hurried to get into line.

When no one was looking, Nicky whispered to Cameron. "I know what you're up to," he said quietly. "You're not too slick, man. If you try to pin this on me, you'll be sorry."

Nicky took his inky thumb and thumped it against Cameron's forehead.

"I'll take care of you later." Nicky got in line with the rest of his class.

"This isn't going very well," Cameron said to Tarann. "Not well at all."

Tarann tugged Cameron's arm.

"Look at the back of his jacket," she whispered.

The back of Nicky's jacket was covered with a wild design.

"He used spray paint," Tarann said.

7
More Trouble

When the final bell for the day rang, Cameron was the first one out of his seat. He pushed through the door and headed home before the rest of his class had picked up their backpacks.

Cameron's heart thumped wildly as he ran. He looked over his shoulder to see if anyone was following him. There was no one in sight.

Wow, Cameron thought. Oscar, Nicky, and the guy by the wall — they're all after me. How did I ever get myself into this mess?

Cameron burst through the front door of his house. He ran up the stairs, two at a time and collided with his father at the top of the stairs.

"Hey, hey," Mr. Thompson said as he grabbed Cameron's arm. "Slow down! Is someone after you?"

"Just about everyone connected to this case," Cameron huffed. He tried to catch his breath.

Mr. Thompson looked out of the upstairs window. "I don't see anyone."

"I didn't want to take any chances," Cameron said. "So I ran really fast, just in case someone was chasing me."

"Why do you have that big, black thumbprint on your forehead?"

"Oh, it's a long story," Cameron said.

"I'm listening," his father said.

Cameron told his father all about his day — even the part about taking the fingerprinting kit. When Cameron finished, his father stood up.

"Come on," his father said. "Let's go."

"Where are we going?"

"To pick up Tarann. Then we'll go to Welberts' SuperStore to get those pictures developed," Mr. Thompson said. "I want to compare that thumbprint on the wall with the ones you got from Miguel and Nicky. I also want to see if I recognize the guy you saw near the wall. We need to wrap up this case before you hurt yourself."

Cameron smiled. "I'll go call Tarann."

Tarann was waiting for them on her front porch. She quickly ran to the car and got in. Her mother watched them from the doorway.

Mr. Thompson waved at Mrs. Johnson.

"Thanks for letting Cameron spend the night tonight. We'll be back later," Mr. Thompson said.

"No problem," Mrs. Johnson said. "I fixed an extra-big dinner."

Mrs. Johnson always teased Cameron about how much he ate.

"Mom said she made spaghetti especially for you," Tarann said.

"Cool," Cameron said. He never got tired of spaghetti.

"Here," Tarann said. She dug into her pocket and handed Cameron the roll of film. "I hope the pictures come out okay. Yesterday was the first time I've ever used my new camera. It has a lot of fancy stuff on it so I had a hard time getting it to work."

"They have to come out," Cameron said. "That thumbprint on the wall and the picture of the guy we saw is our only real evidence."

"I can't wait to see whose thumbprint it is," Tarann said.

"Me, too," Cameron said.

He looked out of the window. They were near Miguel's house.

I hope it's not Miguel, Cameron thought. But I have a feeling he knows all about this case. Why else would he act so weird?

"Everybody out," Mr. Thompson said when they reached Welberts'. "I'll get the film developed. You two go talk to the clerk in the paint department."

"Okay, Dad," Cameron said. He followed Tarann down the long aisles. They were near the paint department when Cameron grabbed Tarann's arm. Suddenly, he pulled her to a stop. Then, Cameron pushed her behind a large stack of paper towels.

"Hey, stop pushing!" Tarann said.

"Shush," Cameron whispered. "It's Miguel."

Miguel was carrying a large can. The sleeve of his bright yellow jacket covered most of the writing on it. Cameron could read only one word. Paint.

Miguel got in line and stood behind a woman with a cart full of stuff. It looked like he'd be there for a while.

"Come on," Cameron said quietly. "Let's go talk to the clerk. Maybe this isn't the first time Miguel's bought paint here."

Cameron and Tarann ran down the aisle

toward the paint section. The store clerk was busy stacking up can after can of paint remover.

"Excuse me," Cameron said. "Did you just help a little boy?"

"No," the clerk said angrily. "But it might have saved me a lot of work if I had. He knocked over this display of paint remover. Then he took off like he was scared to death."

"Did he pick up any spray paint?" Tarann asked.

"I don't know," the clerk said. "The spray paint's in the next aisle."

"Did he take a can of paint remover?" Cameron asked.

"It's hard to say," the clerk answered.

"Have you ever seen him around here before?" Tarann asked.

"Maybe," the clerk said. "A lot of kids come in here to buy stuff. Look, I don't have time for any more questions. I need to get back to work."

"Thanks for your help," Cameron said.

"Sure thing." He finished stacking the last can. Instead of the display being a triangle, it was now flat across the top.

"Didn't you have one can at the very top?" Cameron asked. "It looks kind of strange like that."

"I guess I did," the clerk said. He walked down the aisle and got another can out of a box. He placed it on top of the rest of the cans.

"Yeah, that's the way I had it."

Cameron nodded. "Let's go, Tarann. I think I've figured out this case."

Cameron and Tarann peeked down the aisle. Miguel was gone.

"He must have gotten into another line," Cameron said.

"I guess so," Tarann said. "I should have watched him while you talked to the clerk."

"It doesn't matter," Cameron said. "All I need to do now is compare thumbprints. Then I'll be able to tell Mr. Garcia who spray painted the wall."

"Great," Tarann said. "Let's go see if the pictures are ready."

Cameron and Tarann ran over to the photo counter. Mr. Thompson was paying for the pictures.

"How did they come out?" Tarann asked.

"Let me see them, Dad," Cameron said.

"Hold on," Mr. Thompson said. "I haven't had a chance to look at them myself. Let's go sit in the snack area."

Cameron, Tarann, and Mr. Thompson slid into a booth. Mr. Thompson eagerly opened up the package of photos.

"Oh, no," Mr. Thompson said as he quickly flipped through the photos. "I don't believe this."

He spread the pictures out on the table. There was photo after photo of two small, blurry fingers. Tarann's hand had been in front of the camera lens the whole time.

"Oh, no!" cried Tarann. "I'm so sorry. I was trying to get as close to the wall as I could. I wanted to make sure I got that double zero and the thumbprint. I guess I didn't notice my fingers were in the way."

"Wait a minute," Mr. Thompson said. "These two pictures came out pretty well." Mr. Thompson looked at the pictures closely. "Is this the guy who told you to stay away from the wall?"

Cameron and Tarann looked at the picture.

"Yeah," Cameron said. "That's him. At least we have pictures of one suspect."

"I'm afraid not," Mr. Thompson said. "This is Bill Patterson. He's my new partner on the gang unit. He looks like a teenager. That's why we assign him to the gang investigations."

"There goes my case," Cameron said. "No thumbprints to match, the wall's been sandblasted, and the only good pictures out of thirty-six shots are of a police officer."

8
Case Closed

It was quiet in the car on the way home. The sunlight had faded. The streetlights were coming on.

Cameron was slumped down in his seat. Thirty-six pictures and not one of the mysterious thumbprint. What a day.

"I'm sorry, Cameron," Tarann said quietly.

Cameron looked at Tarann and rolled his eyes.

"I said I was sorry," Tarann said. "I'm a scientist, not a photographer."

"You've got that right," Cameron said. Suddenly, a flash of yellow caught Cameron's eye. He straightened up and looked out the window. "Hey, there goes Miguel."

"Maybe he's on his way home," Mr. Thompson said.

"He doesn't live down that street," Cameron said.

"Let's see where he's going," Tarann said. "Maybe he's going to spray paint another wall."

Mr. Thompson turned down the street. Miguel's bright yellow jacket bobbed in and out of the streetlight.

"I wonder what he's up to," Mr. Thompson said.

"I know what he's doing," Cameron said excitedly. "He was buying paint remover at Welberts', not spray paint! Mr. Murray said it looked like someone spray painted the wall and then changed their mind and tried to wipe it off. I'll bet that Miguel was the one trying to clean off the wall."

"Why would Miguel go to all the trouble

to spray paint the wall and then try to remove the paint?" Tarann asked.

"Miguel's not the spray painter," Cameron said. "I'll bet one of Miguel's brothers is the spray painter. Miguel cleans the walls so his brother doesn't get into trouble again! Let's follow him, Dad."

Mr. Thompson cut off the headlights. He slowly followed Miguel down a narrow street. Miguel stopped. A wall blocked off the end of the street.

"Look at that," Cameron said.

The wall was covered with graffiti. Someone was painting something near the edge. It was Oscar!

Mr. Thompson grabbed his police flashlight and quickly got out of the car.

"Hold it right there, you two," Mr. Thompson said. He shined the light down the dark street. The light flashed over Oscar's and Miguel's frightened faces. Cameron and Tarann got out of the car and ran down the street.

"I wasn't doing anything," Oscar said.

"You're not telling the truth, Oscar," Cameron said. "I know that Miguel bought a can of paint remover tonight. He was going to try to clean off the graffiti you've been writing."

Oscar looked surprised. IIe stared at Miguel.

"I didn't want you to get into any more trouble," Miguel said. "I've been taking your spray paint and hiding it in my backpack. I've even been staying up late every night to follow you. I didn't want to have to move again because of you — I like it here. That's why I tried to scrub the paint off the walls."

"So that's why you had paint all over your hands the first day we met," Cameron said.

"I didn't have time to get it all off," Miguel said. "I forgot about his tag. I should have cleaned that off first."

"I can't believe you did that, Miguel," said Oscar, staring at his shoes.

"Now I remember you, Oscar," Mr.

Thompson said. "I knew I'd seen your face before. Miss Ware, your probation officer in Houston, called me about you. She sent me your picture and your police record."

"I'm not in a gang now," Oscar said. "I just like drawing stuff and tagging walls."

"He draws on everything," Miguel explained. "He even paints on my books and school supplies."

"So that's how your notebook got covered with all that weird stuff," Cameron said. "Oscar did it."

Miguel nodded. Mr. Thompson shined his flashlight over the wall. Oscar had painted a huge rainbow and a flying unicorn. Cameron hated to admit it, but it was beautiful. Then the flashlight beam hit the corner of the wall. A red double zero with a thumbprint in the middle could clearly be seen.

"Hold up your thumbs, Oscar," Tarann said.

Oscar slowly held up his thumbs. The left thumb was clean. The right one was bright red.

"Looks like this solves the Spray Paint Mystery," Cameron said.

"Okay, everyone," Mr. Thompson said. "Get in the car. I'm going to drop you two off at Tarann's. Then I'm going to take Miguel and Oscar home. I need to talk with their parents."

"My dad doesn't live with us," Miguel said.

"Then I'll talk with your mother," Mr. Thompson said. "After we finish talking, I'm going to work. I need to file a case-closed report now that the Spray Paint Mystery is solved." He smiled at Cameron. "Good work, Detective Thompson."

"You too, Detective Dad," Cameron said.

Oscar slumped down in the seat, angrily glaring at Mr. Thompson. The look on his face frightened Cameron. It didn't seem to bother his dad at all.

"Tell your parents that I'm sorry we're so late," Mr. Thompson said when they reached Tarann's house. "You both did a great job."

"Thanks, Mr. Thompson," Tarann said.

"I'll pick you up tomorrow morning, Cameron."

"And don't forget. Tomorrow's Career Day, Dad."

"Thanks for reminding me," Mr. Thompson said. "I'll see you in the morning."

"Bye, Dad," Cameron said. "Thanks for everything. See you, Miguel. Later, Oscar."

"Yeah, later," Oscar mumbled. He didn't look at Cameron or Tarann. Miguel smiled and waved good-bye.

Tarann rang the doorbell and Mr. Johnson answered the door. "Come on in. You're mother's in the kitchen. We were getting worried."

"Mr. Thompson said to apologize to you for being so late," Tarann said.

"We were on official police business," Cameron explained.

"Official what?" asked Mrs. Johnson. Tarann and Cameron began talking at the same time about solving the mystery.

Mr. Johnson held up his hands. "Hold it.

Hold it. Let's sit down. I want to hear all about this."

"I put your dinners in the oven to keep them warm," Mrs. Johnson said. "I'll get the plates."

"Now," Mr. Johnson said. "Let's hear about your adventure."

"I can explain everything, Mr. and Mrs. Johnson," Cameron said.

"Go right ahead," Mrs. Johnson said.

Cameron told them all about the Spray Paint Mystery.

"So you see," Cameron finished, "Miguel was never guilty. He was just trying to keep Oscar from getting into trouble again. I can't wait to get to school tomorrow. I want to tell Mr. Murray and Mr. Garcia what happened tonight."

"Speaking of school," Mrs. Johnson said. "It's time for you two to go to bed. I've already pulled out the sleeper sofa for you, Cameron. Go on to bed."

"Good night, Cameron," Mr. Johnson said.

"Good night," Tarann said. "Sorry about those awful pictures."

"No problem," Cameron said. "Good night, everyone."

Cameron got ready for bed, snuggling down between the blankets. All in all, it had been a pretty good day. He'd learned a lot. Cameron thought about Miguel and Oscar — he had always wanted a brother. He wondered if he would try to protect his brother the way Miguel looked out for Oscar. Cameron thought he probably would.

Cameron rolled over. He tried to find a comfortable spot on the sleeper sofa. He learned one thing tonight that he would never forget. He would never let Tarann take pictures again. He smiled to himself. Thirty-six blurry pictures! Thirty-four of them were of the fingers on her left hand. He couldn't believe it!

He closed his eyes. A sudden thought made him open them again. If Nicky wasn't guilty, why was he acting so strangely?

That was one part of this case Cameron couldn't figure out. Oh, well, he'd work on it at school tomorrow. Maybe Nicky's behavior was another mystery that needed to be solved.

9
Career Day

Cameron walked with his dad to the gym.
Today was the Career Day assembly. Class
after class filed down the hallway.

"We're supposed to sit on stage, Dad."
Cameron said, pointing to the door that led
to the stage.

"Cameron, wait!" Tarann grabbed his
arm.

"Hi," Cameron said. "What's up?"

"I want to take a picture of you and your
dad," Tarann said. "I stayed up for hours

last night reading the instruction book for my new camera."

"Oh, brother," Cameron said.

"Come on, Cameron," Mr. Thompson said. "Smile and say spray paint."

"Spray paint," Cameron said. Tarann took their picture.

"Thanks," Tarann said. "As soon as I get the pictures developed, I'll give you one."

"Okay," Cameron said. Tarann ran to get in line with the rest of her class.

"I hope she doesn't give us more pictures of her fingers," Mr. Thompson said. "We already have plenty."

Cameron laughed. "I'm going to the bathroom, Dad. I'll be back in a minute."

"Hurry," Mr. Thompson said. "The program is about to begin."

Cameron pushed through the bathroom doors. Mr. Murray was putting soap in the dispenser. He smiled when he saw Cameron.

"So," Mr. Murray said, "Mr. Super Detective solves the case."

"How did you find out about it so fast?" Cameron asked.

"I saw your dad in the hall. He told me everything. Congratulations."

"Thanks," Cameron said, smiling.

"I hear Oscar has been put on graffiti cleanup for a whole year. That should keep him busy."

"I hope so," Cameron said. "That was his mother's idea. I told Dad that Mrs. Carter needed help with the scenery for the school play, so Dad's going to talk to her about it. Oscar really is a good artist, you know. I think he'd like painting scenery."

"I hope so," Mr. Murray said. "It took hours to clean that wall behind the gym. Thanks again for your help. If I run across any more cases, you'll be the first to know. See you later."

"Thanks, Mr. Murray," Cameron said. He caught a glimpse of himself in the mirror. His hair looked like a lumpy pillow. He really needed a haircut big time.

Worse, he had to introduce his father to

the entire school. That made Cameron nervous. What if he got up to talk and made a fool out of himself? His stomach was starting to hurt.

Cameron turned on the water and splashed a handful on his face. The door to the bathroom swung open. Someone handed him a paper towel.

"Thanks," Cameron said. He mopped his face dry.

He looked in the mirror. Nicky Viceroy and Oscar Oliveras stared back at him.

Cameron could feel beads of sweat popping out on his forehead. Nicky and Oscar circled around him. Cameron looked at the door. There was no way he could get out of there.

"We want to talk to you," Nicky said.

"Yeah," Oscar said. "We've got something we want to say."

"W-what," Cameron said. His tongue refused to work and his knees were knocking together.

Oscar and Nicky looked at each other.

"Is anyone else around?" Oscar asked.

"I don't think so," Nicky said.

"Okay," Oscar said. "Let's get on with it."

Cameron was terrified. He had to hold on to the sink to keep from falling down.

Oscar raised his hand. "Thanks for everything, man. Give me five."

"Yeah," Nicky said. "Thanks."

"Thanks for what?" Cameron asked, surprised. "What's going on?"

"Well," Oscar said, "your dad said I should thank you for getting me the job with Mrs. Carter. I'm going to be helping Nicky with the scenery."

"I'm sorry about everything," Nicky said. "I was mad at you at first. I thought you were the one who was doing the spray painting. I didn't know you were working on a case. I like your dad. He's helped me a lot. I didn't want you to do anything that would make him look bad."

"So that's why you were acting so funny," Cameron said. "I thought maybe *you* were doing the spray painting."

"I only spray paint on paper now," Nicky said. "I'm through tagging."

"Me, too," Oscar said. "My mom says that I have to help clean off graffiti for a whole year."

"Yeah," Cameron said. "I heard."

"Your dad made me come here today so I could apologize to the whole school," Oscar said. "He also wants me to warn the kids about hanging out with gangs. I'm all right with that. I don't want to get into any more trouble."

"I'm glad, man," Cameron said.

"He wants me to warn the kids, too," Nicky said. "We're sitting on the stage next to you. You were taking too long. So your dad sent us to find you."

"I'm nervous about talking in front of the whole school," Cameron said.

"You don't have to say very much," Nicky said. "Everyone knows your dad's a good guy. That's all you've got to say."

"Don't be scared, little brother," Oscar said. "We've got your back."

99

"Thanks," Cameron said.

The three boys went onstage and took their seats near Mr. Thompson.

"Where have you been?" Mr. Thompson whispered. "I was getting worried."

"I'm sorry," Cameron said. "I was talking to Oscar and Nicky."

"Is everything okay?"

"Everything's fine," Cameron said. He smiled at Nicky and Oscar. They smiled back.

"Now we'll have Cameron Thompson introduce his Career Day guest," Mrs. Sutton said.

Cameron nervously walked up to the mike. The gym was full. Some of the teachers had to stand along the walls. Cameron looked back at his dad. He smiled at Cameron and nodded his head. Nicky and Oscar gave him the thumbs-up. Suddenly, Cameron didn't feel nervous any more.

"I brought someone very special with me to Career Day," Cameron said. "He's a police detective and he also works with the

city's gang unit. I want to be just like him when I grow up. Give it up for my dad, Detective Richard Thompson."

Everyone clapped loudly. Cameron sat down between Nicky and Oscar. He smiled all the way through his dad's speech. Then he listened as Nicky and Oscar told their stories. He looked at the other kids to see if they were listening, too. They were. Tarann smiled at Cameron and waved. Cameron waved back. It was nice to have the smartest kid in the whole third grade for a friend — even if she did take rotten pictures.

Then Cameron saw Miguel sitting out in the crowd. He gave Miguel two thumbs-up. Miguel smiled back. He had something in his hand. He held it up. It was an *empanada*. Cameron smiled. Third grade wasn't so bad after all.